First published in Great Britain in 2004 by Bloomsbury Publishing Plc
38 Soho Square, London, W1D 3HB

Text and illustrations copyright © Rosalind Beardshaw 2004
The moral right of the author/illustrator has been asserted

A CIP catalogue record of this book is available from the British Library

ISBN 0 7475 6473 6

Printed in Hong Kong/China

1 3 5 7 9 10 8 6 4 2

All papers used by Bloomsbury Publishing are natural, recyclable products made
from wood grown in sustainable, well-managed forests.
The manufacturing processes conform to the environmental regulations of the country of origin.

Grandpa's Surprise

Rosalind Beardshaw

BLOOMSBURY
CHILDREN'S
BOOKS

Grandpa and Stanley and Bert the dog were looking out of the window when Jack whizzed past on his new tricycle.

'La la la'

They went outside to watch Jack.
'Ooh,' said Stanley, 'I like your new
tricycle. Can I have a go please?'

'I'll think
about it,'
said Jack.

Jack cycled up and down the path. Grandpa and Stanley and Bert waited.

'I've thought about it,' said Jack.

'Yes?' said Stanley.

'No!' said Jack.

'Come on, Stanley. I know something that will cheer you up. Let's go to the shed,' smiled Grandpa.

Stanley and Grandpa and Bert
went to the shed. Grandpa
started to rummage around.
Stanley was still sulking.

'Perfect,' said Grandpa, as he
pulled out an old wooden
crate.

'What for?' asked Stanley.

'You'll see,' said Grandpa.

Then Grandpa dragged out Stanley's old pram.

'Now then, Stanley, help me take the wheels off this,' said Grandpa.

'OK,' said Stanley.

'Screw that on nice and tight,' said Grandpa.

'Righty-oh!' said Stanley.

'Finishing touches,' said Grandpa.
'It looks brilliant,' said Stanley.

'In we get, Stanley. We'll wear these just in case!' said Grandpa.
'Wheeeee!' shrieked Stanley.

Jack came over to them.
'Do you want a go on my tricycle
now, Stanley?' asked Jack.

'I'll think about it!' said Stanley,
and off they went.

When they came back, Stanley said, 'I've thought about it.'

'Yes?' said Jack.

'No!' said Stanley.

'Oh,' said Jack.

'But you can come on
the go-kart with us!'
said Stanley.

'HOORAY!'

parp
parp